No Such Thing as a Witch

by RUTH CHEW

Illustrated by the author

SCHOLASTIC BOOK SERVICES

NEW YORK · TORONTO · LONDON · AUCKLAND · SYDNEY · TOKYO

Copyright © 1971 by Ruth Chew. All rights reserved. Published by Scholastic
Book Services, a division of Scholastic Magazines, Inc.

13 12 11 10 9 8 7 6 5 4 3   9/7 0 1 2 3 4/8

Printed in the U. S. A.   11

To Maggie Baran
who makes the best fudge
in the world

1

"NORA, look! The squirrel is reading a little newspaper!" Tad Cooper pressed his nose against the kitchen window. The gray squirrel on the fence outside held the folded square of paper close to his face.

"Don't be silly, Tad." Nora reached into the refrigerator for the milk. "You'd better eat your breakfast or you'll be late for school."

"But, Nora, he *is* reading a newspaper."

Nora put the milk on the table and went to the window. The squirrel was still sitting on the picket fence holding the paper in front of him. He raised his head and looked over the paper at the two children.

Then he dropped the paper to the ground and scampered along the fence to the telephone pole. He climbed the pole and did a tight-rope walk along the wire to the roof of the candy store on the corner.

Tad went out the kitchen door. He picked up the paper that the squirrel had dropped. Nora followed her brother into the yard.

"Let me see it." Nora reached for the paper.

Tad handed it to her. "It's a card with somebody's name on it," he said.

The card was folded in half like a book or a little newspaper. Nora opened it and read:

MAGGIE BROWN
Cat Care Service
Telephone 179-1429

Just then both children heard a funny cackle. Someone was laughing. Tad looked up at the upstairs window of the house next door. A woman with a round face and curly gray hair was leaning out. "Did you see the squirrel? Isn't he delightful?"

"What was he doing?" asked Tad.

"Reading a newspaper," said the woman. Then she laughed again. "That's my card. I put peanut butter on it for the squirrel."

"Are you Maggie Brown?" asked Tad.

"Yes. I know who you are. You're Tad. And that's Nora. Why don't you come to see me?"

Mrs. Cooper opened the kitchen door. "Hurry, children, you'll be late for school."

Nora looked up at the woman in the window. The woman smiled and waved. Nora waved back and went into the house.

"Who were you waving to?" asked her mother.

"Maggie Brown," said Nora.

"Nora, you mustn't call grown people by their first names. Is that the lady who just moved into the upstairs apartment next door?"

"She must be," said Nora. "She seems to live there. She's a witch."

Mrs. Cooper was busy loading the dishwasher. "There's no such thing as a witch, Nora, and I don't want you to be a nuisance to the neighbors."

"I think Nora's right," said Tad. "Maggie is a witch."

"Finish your breakfast, Tad," said Mrs. Cooper.

2

WHEN Nora came home from school her mother met her at the door. "Nora," said Mrs. Cooper, "there's something the matter with Skipper. He won't come in out of the yard. And he's barking so much I'm afraid the neighbors will call the police."

"I'll get him in, Mother." Nora put down her books and went out into the back yard. The fuzzy little brown dog was sitting in the middle of the patch of grass and staring up at Maggie Brown's window. When Skipper saw Nora he wagged his tail, but when Nora went over to him he backed up. He kept just out of Nora's reach. His mouth was open, and his tongue was hanging out. He looked as if he were laughing at Nora.

Now Tad came out of the house. He tried to catch Skipper, but the dog managed to dodge him too.

"Hee, hee, hee!" There was that cackle again. Nora looked up to see Maggie Brown at her window.

Maggie put her hand over her mouth as if to stop herself from laughing. Then she called down, "Skip, stop that teasing and go in the house."

Skipper stopped dodging at once and trotted to the back door.

"How did you make him do that, Maggie?" asked Tad.

Maggie Brown smiled. "It's a trick," she said. "I have lots of them. When are you going to come to see me?"

"Can I come now?" asked Tad.

"Sure. Come on." Maggie stepped back and closed the window.

Nora turned to Tad. "Can't you see she's trying to lure you into her house? You don't know what she'll do to you in there. Don't go, Tad."

"I want to go," Tad said. "It's an adventure. I'm not afraid, even if you are."

3

NORA sat down to do her homework, but she kept thinking about Tad.

At supper time Tad had not come home. "Where is Tad?" asked Mrs. Cooper.

"Next door with Maggie Brown," Nora said.

"*Mrs.* Brown is what you call her," said Nora's mother. "Please, Nora, go next door and tell Tad to come home."

Nora wanted very much to go to see

Maggie Brown, but at the same time she was afraid of what might happen to her in the witch's house. There was no use telling her mother about it. Her mother didn't believe in witches. Maybe if Nora had a good luck charm it would keep her safe. She remembered the old horseshoe her father used as a paperweight on his desk. She went to get it.

Nora climbed the stoop of the brownstone house next door. Like many houses in Brooklyn, it looked just like all the others on the block. But instead of one doorbell like Nora's house it had two. Nora pressed the upstairs bell.

While she waited, Nora stroked the horseshoe. Nobody answered the bell. Nora pressed it again.

Almost at once the door opened a very little crack. A bright green eye looked out.

"Come in quickly," said Maggie Brown. "I don't want Henry to escape." She grabbed Nora's arm and pulled her into the house. The door slammed shut behind them.

Maybe Henry is a boy the witch has caught, thought Nora.

She looked around the little front hall. "I just came to tell Tad to come home," she said. "Where is he?"

"Upstairs," said Maggie Brown. "Come on up." She led the way. Nora followed, holding tight to the horseshoe.

At the top of the stairs Maggie turned to the right and went down the long hall to the kitchen at the back of the house. Tad was sitting on the floor wiggling a string in front of a cream-colored Siamese cat.

She's enchanted him already, thought Nora. She knew Tad hated cats.

"Look at Henry. He's more than a hundred years old," said Tad.

"Really?" Nora went over to the cat.

"Maggie says he's lived for twenty people years, and one people year is like seven cat years," Tad said.

Just then something cold and wet touched Nora's knee. She looked down to see a graceful little dog with large brown eyes looking up at her. It looked more like a deer than a dog. Nora patted the dog's smooth head, and it slowly wagged its long tail.

"She's an Italian greyhound," said Tad.

"How can she be a greyhound?" Nora said. "She's not gray. She's brown. What's her name?"

"Taffy," said Maggie Brown. "Come and see the rest of the family." She led Nora into a small bedroom. A ragged green parakeet sat on a perch. There was a black lizard on the floor. He was about two feet long and very ugly. The lizard stuck out his forked tongue at Nora.

Nora stepped back into the hall. "I have to go," she said. "Mother wants us home for supper."

Maggie bent over to stroke the lizard. "I'm sorry you can't stay. I wanted to give you some fudge. Never mind. You can have some to take home."

Nora went to the kitchen to get Tad.

Maggie gave each of them a piece of fudge.

Nora said, "Thank you."

And then she heard Tad say, "Can't I have two pieces, Maggie?"

The witch looked at him.

"Oh please, Maggie. It's such good fudge."

Maggie smiled. "Promise you'll save one piece for tomorrow."

"I promise," Tad said.

Maggie gave him another piece. "Here's another one for you too, Nora. Remember, don't eat both pieces tonight. Run along now. Your mother will be angry with me." She giggled as if she didn't care in the least.

Nora could hear her still cackling away as she and Tad ran down the stairs to the front door.

4

MRS. COOPER was angry because Tad and Nora were late for supper. "Nora, I told you to tell Tad to come home, not to stay there yourself."

She was not happy about the fudge either. "Too many sweets are bad for you," she said.

Nora had already decided not to eat the candy. She was sure it was enchanted.

Tad wanted to eat a piece before supper. Mrs. Cooper took all the fudge and put it in the kitchen to save for later.

After supper Mr. Cooper went into the kitchen. Nora saw him reach for a piece of fudge. "Don't eat it, Daddy! It's enchanted!"

Nora's father laughed. "That's the best excuse for keeping it all to yourself I ever heard." He popped a piece into his mouth. "Nothing wrong with this fudge. It's the best I ever tasted."

He was going to take another piece when Tad came into the kitchen. "Daddy!" said Tad. "That's *my* candy!" Tad grabbed the biggest piece and stuffed it into his mouth.

Mr. Cooper put his hand in his pocket, but it seemed to Nora that he couldn't take his eyes off the fudge. Then he looked around. "Where's Skip? I haven't seen him this evening."

Mrs. Cooper was bringing the dirty plates out from the dining room. "That dog!" she said. "He really must be taught to obey. I can't get him to do anything I want him to."

"He's just thinking for himself," said Mr. Cooper. Skipper came into the kitchen looking for after-dinner scraps. Mr. Cooper gave him a piece of meat from one of the plates.

"Oh, John!" said Mrs. Cooper. "How can I train him not to beg if you do that? I have a hard enough time keeping the children from giving him leftovers. I never thought *you*'d start doing it." She began to put the dishes in the dishwasher.

It was strange, thought Nora. Daddy almost never paid any attention to the dog. He was always too busy. Suddenly Nora had an idea. "Tad," she said, "did Maggie give you any fudge when you were in her house?"

Tad was sitting on the floor with his

arm around Skipper who was licking Tad's nose. He didn't seem to hear Nora. She went over to him. "Tad, answer me. Did you eat any fudge when you were next door?"

Tad looked at her. "Fudge? Yes. Before Maggie introduced me to Henry. Listen to Skipper."

Nora could hear the dog making the little snuffling whistling noise he always made if anybody petted him. She gave him a pat.

"Nora," said Tad, "can't you hear? He's talking!"

"Of course he is, silly."

"But, Nora, I can understand him. Can't you?"

Nora stared at Tad. He seemed to mean what he said.

The idea Nora had was getting clearer. She looked at her father. There were still two pieces of fudge on the plate. He reached for one of them.

Nora's mother saw him too. "John, that's the children's candy! Besides, you're getting fat."

Mr. Cooper looked up. "One more won't hurt," he said.

Nora grabbed the two pieces of candy and ran out of the room. What was it the witch had said? Save one for tomorrow!

5

UPSTAIRS in her room, Nora put the two pieces of fudge in her dresser drawer. She sat on the edge of the bed and tried to think. She was sure the fudge was magic, but she had to prove it. There was only one way.

Nora opened the dresser drawer and took one piece of fudge. She nibbled a corner of it — delicious! Once she had started, Nora couldn't stop until it was all gone.

There was a faint scratching noise in her closet. It must be a mouse, thought Nora. I wonder if Mother set that terrible trap again.

Nora's mother hated mice. All the houses on the block were attached to each other, and the mice ran between the walls from one house to another. Nora's mother put traps under the radiators in all the rooms.

Nora got down on her hands and knees and carefully pulled the trap from under the radiator. It was set and baited with a piece of bacon. Nora hit the trap with her hairbrush to release the spring. Then she took the bacon out and poked it into the closet through the crack under the door.

"I hope the mouse enjoys the bacon," she said to herself. "Now, what was I going to do? Oh yes, the fudge." Nora took the other piece of fudge out of her drawer and put it into her mouth. It tasted even better than the first piece.

Nora heard the scratching again. And now she also heard a very small voice. It was so small Nora wondered if she had imagined it. No, there it was again. "Let me out," said the voice.

Nora opened the closet door.

A fat gray mouse with bright eyes and large pink ears was sitting in the doorway licking his whiskers. When he saw Nora he didn't scurry away as the mice usually did. Instead he sat up like a squirrel, holding up his little paws in front of him.

"That was very good bacon," said the mouse. "Is there any more?"

Nora was too surprised to answer.

The mouse shouted as if he thought she was deaf, "I said, is there any more bacon?"

"Maybe Mother put some in the other

traps," Nora said, "but don't go near them. You'll be killed."

"Well, it was nice of you to give me that piece," said the mouse. "Now I suppose I'll have to look around next door. I don't really like going there. That cat is a mean one."

"You mean Henry? He looked like a nice cat to me," Nora said.

"No cat is a nice cat," said the mouse. "Maybe I shouldn't go over there after all. You never know what will happen when you eat the food there."

Nora remembered the fudge. "Is that why I can understand you, because I ate Maggie's fudge?"

"I shouldn't be surprised," said the mouse. He looked around. "Do you have anything else to eat?"

"I could get you a slice of bread," said Nora.

"Never mind," said the mouse. "I can usually get that for myself. Thank you anyway, and good-by." He dived into a crack under the baseboard in the closet. Nora was alone again.

She sat on her bed and rested her chin in her hand. "It's the fudge, all right," she said to herself. "One piece makes you fond of animals. Two pieces make you understand their language. I'll have to find Skipper and talk to him. Maybe he'll tell me what he did with my bedroom slipper."

6

NORA found Skipper in the living room. He was curled up on the sofa beside Nora's father who was reading the newspaper.

"Skipper," said Nora. "I want you to show me where you hid my bedroom slipper."

Skipper rested his chin on his paws and rolled his eyes upward. "It's not often I'm allowed on the sofa," he said. "Don't bother me."

"You can come back later," said Nora.

Nora's father put down his paper. "I can't think with all your jabber, Nora. Run along and leave the poor dog in peace." He gave Skipper a pat on the head.

"Come on, Skip," begged Nora.

Skipper didn't move.

"Be a good dog, Skip. I'll take you for a walk tomorrow."

"I'm comfortable," said Skipper.

"Nora!" said Mr. Cooper. "I told you to leave the dog alone. Do as you're told."

Nora went to find Tad. She met her mother coming out of the kitchen. "Where's Tad, Mother?"

"I sent him to bed. He was giving that dog the roast beef I wanted to use for sandwiches. He said Skipper told him he was tired of dog food." Mrs. Cooper went into the living room. Nora heard a yelp, and Skipper went racing past her with his tail between his legs. There was the sound of angry voices in the living room.

Nora put her fingers in her ears. Now her parents were quarreling. She hated this more than anything else in the world.

Nora had to do something. She slipped out the front door and ran next door to ring Maggie Brown's bell. She was in such a rush that she forgot to take the horseshoe.

Nora held her finger on the button and rang and rang.

The door opened, and Maggie stood in the doorway. "Why, Nora," she said, "what's the matter?"

Nora was crying.

"Come in, dear," said the witch. "Maybe I can help you."

Nora went up the dark stairs. Taffy met her at the top and offered her a paw.

Nora shook the paw. She walked down the hall to the kitchen. The cat, Henry, was sitting in the middle of the floor. "Oh, it's you again," he said. "Where's your brother?"

"He was sent to bed," said Nora. "That's part of the reason why I came back here."

Maggie had come into the room. She bustled around, tidying up the kitchen just like a neat little housewife.

Nora was not fooled. She could see that the supper dishes were still in the sink, and the floor needed sweeping. Besides, the whole apartment smelled like a zoo.

"Maggie," said Nora, "please help me." Suddenly she wasn't at all afraid of this little witch. She had the feeling Maggie was almost afraid of *her*. At any rate the witch seemed to want to be friends.

Maggie sat down and pulled out a chair for Nora. She leaned across the kitchen table. "Did I do something wrong?" she asked. "I didn't mean to. Don't be angry with me, Nora."

Nora felt sorry for the witch. Maggie looked so unhappy. Nora wasn't angry any more. "Maybe you didn't mean to," she said, "but you caused an awful lot of trouble. Tad was sent to bed for giving Skipper the roast beef Mother wanted for sandwiches, and now Daddy and Mother are fighting because Daddy let Skip sit on the sofa. And it really is all because of your fudge."

"It's not my fault," said Maggie. "I told you not to eat more than one piece, but it sounds as if somebody had two. And I don't know what your father has to do with it."

"He took one of Tad's," said Nora. "And you gave Tad a piece earlier in the day." She didn't tell the witch that she herself had eaten two pieces.

"Did I?" said the witch. "Oh, yes, that was because he said he didn't like cats, and Henry did so want to make friends. I hoped it would have worn off before he ate the next piece."

"Worn off!" said Nora. "What do you mean?"

"The magic of the fudge lasts only as long as the effect of an aspirin."

"You mean that by tomorrow we'll all be just the way we were before we ate the fudge?"

"Yes," said Maggie. "There's nothing to worry about."

The kitchen door squeaked, and the big ugly lizard walked into the room. Nora thought he looked sad. She stood up and went over to him. And then the lizard stuck out his forked tongue and said, "Do I make you think of a snake? I can't help it. I wish I looked like a rabbit, or a bird, or anything people want for a pet."

"I bought him from Gimbel's pet shop," said Maggie. "Poor thing, no one else wanted him."

Nora stroked the lizard's smooth side.

"You won't like me once the fudge wears off," said the lizard.

"What's your name?" asked Nora.

"Lucifer," he answered.

"I'm going to call you Lew for short," Nora said. She patted him again. Then she turned to Maggie. "I'd better go before Mother starts to look for me."

Maggie took her downstairs and let her out by the front door.

7

THE next day, Saturday, Nora still couldn't find her bedroom slipper. Skipper was sitting just inside the back door, waiting to be let out. "Where's my slipper?" Nora asked him. The dog just whined and scratched at the door as if he didn't understand.

The magic has worn off, Nora thought. She opened the door for Skipper and went to find Tad. He was in his room, looking in a box of nuts and bolts.

"Tad," Nora asked, "did Skipper really talk to you last night?"

Tad found the screw he was looking for. "I thought he did," he said slowly. "Now I'm not sure. But I don't know why I gave him the roast beef. I sure got in trouble for that."

"Remember the fudge?" said Nora. "I thought it was enchanted, and I was right. One piece makes you like animals. Two makes you understand their language."

"Then why can't I understand Skipper this morning?"

"The magic only lasts as long as an aspirin. It's worn off."

"How do you know all this?" Tad wanted to know.

Nora told Tad all that had happened the night before. "I never did get Skip to tell me what he did with my bedroom slipper," she finished.

"Let's go get some more fudge from Maggie," Tad said.

Nora shook her head. "You can't just *ask* for it."

"Why not?" asked Tad.

"Because it's rude," Nora said.

"Well, I'll act as if I don't like her cat, and she'll give me some. I'll pretend to eat it. But I'll save it till later. Henry's an O.K. cat. I don't need magic to like him."

"Maybe I can work the same trick with that lizard," Nora said.

Tad put away the box of nuts and bolts. "Let's go next door."

They went downstairs and were about to go out when their mother stopped them. "Where are you going?"

"To see Mrs. Brown," said Nora.

"You know I don't like you bothering the neighbors," Mrs. Cooper said.

Tad held up the screw. "I promised to fix Maggie's bird cage."

"*Mrs. Brown!* Not *Maggie,* Tad," said his mother. "Well, run along then, but don't stay longer than you need to."

Tad and Nora went next door to ring the bell.

There was no answer. Tad rang again. Still no one came to the door. The children turned to go. They met Mrs. Hastings coming up the steps with a bag of groceries. Mrs. Hastings owned the house. She lived on the ground floor.

"We're looking for Mrs. Brown," said Tad.

Mrs. Hastings put her shopping bag on the stoop. "She's not in," she said. "She goes out early every morning to take care of her cat-service customers. She feeds the cats when their owners are out of town. She won't be home until this afternoon."

"Can I help carry your groceries, Mrs. Hastings?" asked Nora.

"Thank you, Nora. Would you put

them on the kitchen table, please." Mrs. Hastings opened the door and led the children through the house to the kitchen. The house was dark and neat. Mrs. Hastings lived alone. She looked out of her kitchen window into the back yard.

Suddenly she rapped on the kitchen window. "Scat, scat!" said Mrs. Hastings. "Lately the yard is always full of cats," she said in an angry voice.

Tad and Nora looked out to see two cats sitting on the grass in Mrs. Hastings' yard. One was black and white and one had gray stripes. Both cats were looking up at Maggie Brown's window. Mrs. Hastings banged on her window again. The cats did not move. She took a broom and went out the back door.

Tad and Nora followed her into the yard. "Good-by, Mrs. Hastings," said Tad. He and Nora climbed the fence into their own yard.

8

AFTER lunch Tad and Nora went to ring Maggie Brown's bell again. This time Maggie opened the door. She smiled when she saw who it was.

"I've got the screw to fix your bird cage," said Tad. He and Nora followed Maggie up the stairs. There was a folding gate at the top, like the ones people use to keep babies from falling downstairs.

"I just put this up," said Maggie. "It's good enough to keep Taffy and Lucifer up here, but I still have to watch Henry."

"Meow!" The cat jumped onto the bannister post at the top of the stairs.

Tad was about to pet him. Then he remembered. He wasn't supposed to like cats.

"Meow!" Henry jumped onto Tad's shoulder.

Nora grabbed the cat. "Tad doesn't like cats," she said. Henry spat at her. He jumped to the floor, shook his hind leg at Nora, and marched away toward the kitchen.

Maggie didn't seem to notice. She was looking at the bird cage. "The stand is wobbly. I'm afraid it will fall over."

Maggie took the parakeet out of the cage. "This is Chatty." She handed the bird to Nora.

Chatty really was strange-looking. One wing was green and shiny, but the other had bare patches and broken feathers.

Nora held the little warm bird in her hand. She could feel its tiny heart beating. How would it feel to have wings, Nora wondered, and then be shut up in a cage.

Something cold touched Nora's leg. She looked down to see the lizard looking up at her with soft brown eyes. Nora just couldn't let the lizard think she didn't like him. She stroked his smooth brown side. The lizard stuck out his forked tongue, and Nora thought that he smiled.

The parakeet fluttered out of Nora's hand and flew onto the top of a door.

Maggie was holding the bird-cage stand while Tad tightened the screw. Only Nora saw Henry the cat make a leap for the bird. She grabbed the cat's tail. Henry snarled and turned his head to bite her. Suddenly the lizard darted forward. Henry was so startled that he backed away, hissing.

Now Maggie turned her head to see what was going on. She hopped on a chair and grabbed the little bird off the top of the door.

The witch shut Chatty back in the cage. "Thank you for fixing the stand, Tad," she said. "Now, how about some fudge?"

Maggie went to the kitchen and came back with a plate of fudge. "Just one piece, now," she said.

Tad took a piece and pretended to put it in his mouth. He moved his mouth as if he were chewing. When the witch turned to offer the fudge to Nora, Tad slipped his piece into his pocket.

Nora took the biggest piece of fudge on the plate. She held it to her mouth and pretended to be nibbling. Nora didn't have a pocket in her dress.

The lizard rubbed his soft side against Nora to remind her that he was there. She stroked him gently with the hand that didn't hold the fudge.

Tad went to look for Henry. He found him in the kitchen, picked him up, and rubbed the cat's stomach. Henry purred loudly.

Maggie came into the kitchen and opened the window. Tad saw her tie a string to a tin pail. She put some cat food in the pail and leaned out the window to lower the pail to the ground. Just then Nora came into the kitchen, followed by the lizard. She went to the window to see what Maggie was doing.

Nora looked down. The black and white cat and the striped gray one were climbing into the pail and gobbling the cat food. Now Nora knew why the cats were always in Mrs. Hastings' yard.

While the witch's back was turned Tad took two more pieces of fudge off the plate on the kitchen table.

As soon as the cats had finished eating, Maggie pulled up the pail with the string and shut the window. "I'll have to get something to feed the pigeons," she said.

Nora wondered if Mrs. Hastings liked pigeons. Nora's mother thought they were dirty birds.

Maggie looked around the messy kitchen. "There's nothing more to do here," she said. "I think I'll pull the feathers out of Chatty's wing."

Nora felt sick. So that was what was wrong with the bird! The cruel witch pulled her feathers out! Nora had begun to like the witch, but she didn't like her now.

Nora wished she had the horseshoe. She was afraid the witch might do something terrible to her. Still she had to speak.

"Maggie — I mean Mrs. Brown," she said. "Please don't hurt the bird."

"It's for her own good," said the witch.

Nora could see that nothing she said would make any difference. Suddenly she couldn't bear to be near the witch. "Tad," she said, "Mother told us not to stay long. Come on home."

Tad went on playing with Henry. Nora took the cat and put him on the floor. She grabbed Tad's hand. "Good-by, Mrs. Brown," she called and dragged Tad out of the kitchen.

"What's the matter, Nora?" asked Tad as she hurried him down the stairs and out the front door.

"Can't you see how wicked she is?" said Nora. "She gets those animals in her power and then she tortures them."

9

Nora ran up to her room and put her piece of fudge in her dresser drawer. "I'm going to save it till I need it," she told Tad when she came back downstairs.

Tad's fudge was still in his pants pocket. His mother was just putting supper on the table. Tad knew she'd take the fudge away if she saw it.

After supper Tad and Nora went up to Nora's room. "There's no need for us to use all the fudge," said Nora. "I can eat two pieces and get Skipper to tell me where he put my bedroom slipper."

"Why can't *I* eat them?" said Tad. "I was the one who swiped the extra pieces."

Nora didn't really want to eat the fudge. It had been in Tad's pants pocket for several hours. "All right," she said, "but promise you won't let Skipper talk you into anything stupid. And don't forget to ask him about my slipper."

Tad took all three pieces of fudge out of his pocket. It was sticky and soft now, but it still tasted better than any other fudge he'd ever had. Tad ate two pieces.

"That's enough," said Nora. But the fudge tasted so good that Tad couldn't stop eating it. He put the third piece in his mouth.

"Now go find Skipper," said Nora, "and ask him what he did with the slipper."

Tad didn't seem to hear. He stretched his neck. Then he carefully licked the stickiness off his hands. He got down on the floor and tried to touch his chin with his foot. After that he put his nose to the crack under Nora's closet door and sniffed.

"That mouse is in there again," he said in a whisper. "Mousie, would you like some bacon?" Tad put his fingers under the closet door and pulled it open.

The fat gray mouse sat in the doorway. He squeaked something, but Nora couldn't understand it. She wished Tad hadn't eaten all his fudge. It would be nice to know what the mouse was saying.

Nora opened her dresser drawer and took out her fudge. It was a very big piece. Maybe it would work like *two* pieces. She was just going to put the fudge in her mouth when Tad reached up and batted it out of her hand.

The next second Tad put his mouth down to the floor and gobbled up the fudge.

"Tad! What are you doing?"

"Meow!"

A big yellow striped cat was in the place where Tad had been a second ago.

The mouse jumped right over the cat's head and ran out the door. The cat turned and streaked after him. Nora heard them go chasing down the stairs. A moment later she heard her mother scream.

Nora ran downstairs. Her father was rushing from the living room to the dining room, trying to swat the cat with his newspaper. A vase had fallen. The flowers were scattered, and a pool of water was soaking into the carpet.

Nora's mother stood in the kitchen doorway waving a dishcloth. The yellow cat raced around in circles after the mouse. Suddenly the mouse ducked under the dining room radiator and disappeared.

The cat tried to hide under the buffet.

Mr. Cooper put down the newspaper. "Who let that cat in, Nora? Take it out of here at once. You remember what I told you the last time!"

"Here, kitty, kitty." Mrs. Cooper was trying to get the cat to come out from under the buffet. The cat moved farther back against the wall.

Skipper was barking in the yard. Mr. Cooper opened the door. Skipper rushed into the dining room and over to the buffet, still barking. The cat meowed loudly. Skipper stopped barking and backed away. All the fuzzy hair on his back stood on end.

"Where is Tad?" said Mr. Cooper. "He'll get the cat out of here. He doesn't like cats any more than I do."

Nora's brain was working again. Things had been happening so fast that she hadn't had time to think. Now she was beginning to understand what was going on. That fourth piece of fudge had turned Tad into a cat.

"I'll get the cat, Daddy," said Nora. She lay on her stomach and pulled the cat out from under the buffet. "Mother," she said, "isn't he a beautiful cat? He must belong to somebody." Nora knew her mother liked cats.

Mrs. Cooper came over and stroked the cat's soft fur. The cat looked at her with big yellow eyes. "Poor thing," said Nora's mother. "I wish we could keep him, but your father hates cats. You'll have to put him outside, Nora. I'm sure he'll find his way home."

"Maybe he's lost, Mother." Nora knew the magic would wear off by morning. "Just let me keep him tonight, and tomorrow we can ask if anybody knows where he belongs."

Nora's mother looked at her father. "Please, John," she said, "I think Nora's right. We ought to keep the cat till we can find out where it belongs."

Mr. Cooper shook his head. "You're just trying to adopt that cat into the family. I want you to put it outdoors right now."

"But, Daddy, it might rain. Didn't you hear the thunder?" Nora held the cat close. "I promise you won't see the cat tomorrow."

"Oh, all right," said Mr. Cooper. "I only wish Tad were here. He'd get rid of that cat fast enough. By the way, where *is* Tad?"

10

WHILE her mother and father were looking all over the house for Tad, Nora took the cat upstairs. She went back into her own room and put the cat on a chair.

"Now you'd better stay there, Tad, or I'll have to put you outdoors." Nora sat on her bed. "It's all your own fault. You were such a pig about that fudge. I wonder why you didn't turn into a pig."

The cat meowed and seemed to be trying to explain, but Nora couldn't understand.

She went on talking to Tad, even

though it seemed like talking to herself because she couldn't understand his answers. "It seems that *three* pieces of fudge made you act like a cat, and *four* made you turn into one. After this you'd better let me take charge of any fudge we get. You have no self-control."

Nora had an idea. Her room was at the front of the house. A little ledge ran under the windows of all the houses on the block. Nora went to her window and opened it. "Tad, climb over to Maggie's window and get some more fudge."

The cat shook his head.

Nora went on. "I suppose you mean you've had enough fudge. But I don't want you to eat it. Just get it, and I'll keep it till we need it."

The cat didn't move.

"Come on, Tad," said Nora, "you've always been a good climber. Just think how good you'll be now that you're a cat."

The cat pricked up his ears.

Nora took the plastic bag her new socks had come in. "Put the fudge in this," she said. The cat held the bag in his mouth. Nora put him on the ledge outside the window. He picked his way along the ledge to Maggie's window. Nora saw him use both paws to shove it open. Then he jumped into the witch's apartment.

"Nora," her mother was calling, "where is Tad? Do you think he's run away because I punished him last night?"

Nora opened her door and went to the head of the stairs. "He went to Mrs. Brown's to get something."

"I hope you children aren't making a nuisance of yourselves next door." Mrs. Cooper went back to finish cleaning up the kitchen.

Nora returned to her room. She decided to do her homework while she was waiting for Tad.

Nora copied all her spelling words three times over. She did examples *A* through *F* on page thirty-six of her arithmetic book. Then she read a chapter in her reader. Tad had still not come back. Nora began to worry.

It shouldn't take so long just to stuff a few pieces of fudge into a plastic bag. Nora went to her window and leaned out. Maggie's window was dark. Suppose the witch had caught Tad? She might be torturing him right now. It was all Nora's fault. She was older than Tad. She never should have sent him to steal the fudge.

Nora knew it was wrong to steal. She decided to take the horseshoe and go and ring Maggie Brown's bell.

She was about to run out of the room when she saw a dark shape crawl out of the witch's window. It crept along the ledge toward Nora.

It was the yellow cat. He was carrying

the plastic bag in his mouth. It was so full of fudge that he could hardly lift it.

As soon as Tad was inside her room Nora took the bag of fudge away from him. She put it in her desk drawer, locked the drawer, and took the key out of the lock. "I don't want you to get into it again," she said.

Tad meowed something.

"I wish I knew what took you so long," Nora said, "but you'll have to tell me tomorrow." She picked up the cat, carried him down the hall to Tad's room, and shut the door.

Before Mrs. Cooper went to bed she opened Tad's door. She found him fast asleep on top of his bedspread. He had all his clothes on and was curled up like a cat.

11

BREAKFAST was late on Sunday morning. The telephone rang just as Mrs. Cooper was sitting down to eat the last waffle. She went to answer the phone. "Hello," she said and then listened for a while. "Yes, of course, if you like. Thank you. It's very nice of you. You can come for them whenever you want to."

Mrs. Cooper came back to the breakfast table. "John," she said, "that was our new neighbor, Mrs. Brown. She wants to take the children to the zoo. No wonder they like her so much. She has a good sense of humor. She said she has an appointment with a bear."

"Well, at least it will keep them out of trouble for the day," said Mr. Cooper. "Are you sure that cat is gone?"

"Yes, he must have gotten out during the night. I can't find him anywhere." Mrs. Cooper took a sip of coffee. "He was a beautiful cat."

Tad grinned. Nora kicked him under the table. "Mother," she said, "I don't want to go to the zoo with Mrs. Brown."

"No," said Tad, "she's a mean old witch."

Mrs. Cooper put down her fork. "I can't understand you children. You spend all your time running over to visit Mrs. Brown, but when she offers to take you to the zoo you don't want to go. Well, you'll have to learn manners some time. I told Mrs. Brown she could take you, so you'll have to go. You'd better change your clothes. Run along."

Nora and Tad went upstairs. "I wonder what the witch is up to," said Nora. "And, by the way, Tad, why did you take so long to get the fudge last night?"

"Henry was telling me the story of his life," said Tad, "and he's terribly old. I was afraid if I didn't listen to it all he'd tell Maggie I was there."

"What was she doing?" asked Nora.

"Watching television," said Tad. "She just sat in front of the set and laughed and laughed. She was watching one of those programs about witches."

Nora went into her room. Tad stood in the doorway. "Why don't we eat some of the fudge so we can understand the animals at the zoo?" he asked.

"I can't trust you with that fudge," Nora said. "You never know when to stop. There's no telling what kind of animal you'd turn into next time. I still don't know why you turned into a cat and not a pig."

"Oh, that's easy," Tad said. "I was thinking about cats. I asked Henry about it. He said you turn into whatever you're thinking about at the time."

"That settles it," Nora said. "We're *not* taking the fudge to the zoo. I'm going to leave it locked up till we need it."

Nora shut the door and got her blue dress out of the closet. The zoo might be fun after all. She'd just have to make sure Maggie didn't play any tricks on them.

12

THE ZOO was in Prospect Park. Maggie Brown took Nora and Tad there on the bus. The sun was shining, and a lot of people were going to the zoo. The bus was crowded. They had to stand for part of the way. Nora wondered why the witch didn't work some magic to get them seats. Tad thought she should have flown them to the zoo on a broom.

When they got to the zoo Maggie stopped the first keeper she saw. "I'm looking for Mr. Perkins."

"You'll find him over in the llama's cage," said the keeper.

Maggie walked over to the llama's cage. "Mr. Perkins," she called, "remember me? Mrs. Rothstein asked me to look in on her bear."

Mr. Perkins put down the shovel he was using. He smiled and came to the gate of the cage. "Of course I remember you, Mrs. Brown," he said. He opened the gate and came out of the cage. "I want to thank you for your advice about that cockatoo. I used to have to hide it every time the inspector came by. He wanted the poor bird destroyed. It looked so terrible. You should see it now."

"What was the matter with it?" asked Tad.

"It was the most raggedy bird you ever saw," said Mr. Perkins. "Mrs. Brown told me to pull out all the broken feathers, and they'd grow in healthy. It seemed like a terrible thing to do, but it was either that or getting rid of the bird."

Maggie Brown was smiling. Nora looked at her. "Is that why you were going to pull out Chatty's feathers?" she asked.

"Yes," said Maggie. "One of my customers gave her to me because she was so scraggly. I've tried every other way I could think of to make those feathers grow, but nothing else worked."

Nora was quiet. She knew that she had been wrong in thinking Maggie was cruel. Now she felt guilty for stealing the fudge.

Mr. Perkins took them to the back gate of the bear's cage, behind the stone cave. The bear came to the gate, and Mr. Perkins gave him a carrot. "Mrs. Rothstein gave the bear to the zoo," Mr. Perkins told the children. "She had him when he was a cub."

Mr. Perkins took them to see his favorite animals. He told them stories of things that had happened in the zoo. And he even took them to his office to show them photographs he had taken of the animals. Nora and Tad had never had such a good time at the zoo.

Maggie Brown seemed to be having just as much fun as Tad and Nora. After they said good-by to Mr. Perkins, she bought them each a balloon on a string. Then they got back on the bus to go home.

13

ALMOST every afternoon after school Tad and Nora went to see Maggie Brown. Sometimes she gave them fudge, but never more than one piece. Nora always made sure Tad ate his. She was afraid of what might happen if he collected three or four pieces. She always ate hers too because it was so delicious and because it seemed the safest thing to do.

Maggie's closets were full of shoes and hats. She no longer wore most of them, and she let Nora play with them. "You can take them home if you like," the witch told Nora.

There was a big box of old beads and earrings without mates on the floor of one of the closets. "You can have any of that stuff you want," said Maggie. At first Nora thought the jewelry might be enchanted, but it never made her disappear or learn how to fly. It was just fun to dress up in.

Tad spent his time making and fixing things. He painted all the doorknobs with glow-in-the-dark paint. And he made a false bottom in the kitchen drawer in case Maggie needed to hide something.

Maggie's kitchen table wobbled. When Tad tried to even up the legs, he made it two inches shorter. Maggie didn't mind.

Meanwhile Maggie's family was getting bigger. There was a baby sparrow that had fallen out of his nest. Maggie put him in a shoe box lined with cotton. Tad was afraid Henry would get him, so he made a little cage for the sparrow.

Maggie found a litter of kittens someone had left in the vacant lot around the corner. She brought them home, and Tad helped make a bed for them. Maggie put a hot water bottle in it to keep the kittens warm. They snuggled against it as if it were their mother. Tad and Nora helped Maggie feed the kittens with an eyedropper. "As soon as they're big enough," she said, "I'll give them to Gimbel's pet shop. I used to work there."

Four pairs of pigeons came to be fed every morning, and the squirrel brought his mate with him to the kitchen window.

Wherever Nora went in Maggie's apartment the lizard went with her. Nora didn't think he was ugly now. She liked his sad brown eyes. And she even liked the way the lizard's forked tongue would suddenly flash out of his mouth. It usually meant that he was excited about something — or glad to see her.

14

ONE afternoon Tad went with Maggie
Brown to the hardware store around the
corner. He helped Maggie choose a new
set of hinges for her kitchen cabinet.
When they came out of the store Tad
noticed a little black cat sitting in front
of the new delicatessen next door.

"That's Whiskers," said Tad. "Doesn't
he belong to Mr. Samuels who used to
have the grocery store here? I wonder
why Mr. Samuels didn't take the cat with
him when he sold the store."

"Whiskers made his home in the store," said Maggie. "He wouldn't be happy anywhere else. Mr. Samuels told me he gave the cat to Mr. Hellman — the man who bought the store."

Maggie went into the delicatessen. Tad followed her.

"Mr. Hellman," said Maggie, "what's old Whiskers doing out on the street?"

"I can't have a dirty animal in my store," said the delicatessen man.

"But Whiskers has never been out of the store."

"He's out now," said Mr. Hellman.

Tad watched the little black cat. It was huddled against the store front, trying to keep out of the way of people passing by.

A big striped tomcat strolled around the corner. He stopped to hiss at little Whiskers who ran under a parked delivery truck.

"He'll get killed!" said Tad. "Please, Mr. Hellman, let him back in the store. He's a clean cat."

"I won't have a cat getting into my salami," said Mr. Hellman. "If you're so fond of the cat you take him."

Maggie pressed her lips together. Her green eyes glinted. She looked hard at the delicatessen man. "I won't be buying anything more from you," she said, "and don't be surprised if rats get into your salami." She took Tad by the hand and marched out of the store.

Outside on the street Maggie stopped to coax Whiskers out from under the truck. Tad scooped him up. "Are you going to keep him, Maggie?"

"I guess I'll have to. Henry won't like it, but I'll keep Whiskers in the living room. Henry can still be king of the kitchen."

After supper Tad told Nora about Whiskers. "Why doesn't Maggie just feed the delicatessen man some of her fudge?" Nora asked.

"It wears off, silly," Tad reminded her.

"Sometimes," Nora said, "I wonder if we dreamed all that stuff about the fudge. Nothing magic happens any more."

"Well, why don't we get out that fudge I swiped and test it?" asked Tad.

"I can't trust you to stop at two pieces," said Nora. "And I'm saving it till we really need it. Now, go do your homework. I still have my arithmetic to do."

15

TAD and Nora were coming home from school. They passed Hellman's delicatessen just as a lady came running out. She was carrying a little boy, and she seemed very upset. "No, no, Tommy. That was *not* a squirrel, and you can't pet it!"

Mr. Hellman came out of the store after the lady. "It won't happen again. I'll get rid of them. I promise." Mr. Hellman caught sight of Tad. "Boy," he said, "come here."

"What do you want, Mr. Hellman?" Tad asked.

"I'll give you a dollar if you bring that cat back."

"You mean Whiskers? I don't think Mrs. Brown will give him back," said Tad.

"Why not?" Mr. Hellman looked angry.

"She wants Whiskers to have a good home," said Tad.

Mr. Hellman looked ready to explode, but he just said, "You tell Mrs. Brown I'll be good to the cat. Now go get it."

Tad and Nora went around the corner and down the street. Tad rang Maggie's bell. When Maggie opened the door, Tad said, "Mr. Hellman wants Whiskers back."

Maggie smiled. "I thought he would."

"You mean you'll *let* him have Whiskers?" said Nora. "Suppose he's mean to him?"

"He won't be," said the witch. "And Whiskers will be happy to be back in his old home. Henry will be happy too. He

hates being kept out of the living room."
Maggie went upstairs to get Whiskers.

Tad took the cat back to the delicatessen. Mr. Hellman forgot to give him the dollar.

Later in the afternoon Nora's mother gave her some money and told her to buy a pound of potato salad for supper. Nora went to the delicatessen. She wanted to see how Whiskers was doing.

The cat was chasing something behind the counter.

Mr. Hellman was busy talking to Mrs. Hastings. Neither of them saw Nora when she came in.

"That Mrs. Brown you have living in your house is ruining the neighborhood," said Mr. Hellman.

"Well, she does have too many animals in that apartment," said Mrs. Hastings. "I've asked her not to feed all the stray cats, but I think she still does. It's very annoying."

"That's not all she does. That woman raises *rats*," said Mr. Hellman.

"Rats! I know she has snakes and birds and dozens of cats, but rats!" Mrs. Hastings shook her head.

"She raises them and puts them in my store," said Mr. Hellman. "She even tried to take my cat away, but I've got him back now. He'll get rid of those rats."

Mrs. Hastings nearly dropped her shopping bag. "Oh, dear, rats! Whatever shall I do?"

"I'll tell you what to do, Mrs. Hastings," said Mr. Hellman. "You call the Department of Health. They'll give her a summons and make her get rid of those animals."

"I will," Mrs. Hastings said. "I'll telephone this afternoon."

Nora didn't wait to hear any more. She ran out of the store. She went to the delicatessen on the next block to get the potato salad.

As soon as she got home Nora told Tad what she had heard. "Now is the time to use that fudge we've been saving," she said. "I'm going to give a piece to Mrs. Hastings. That will make her like animals so much she won't mind how many Maggie has in her apartment. She won't call the Health Department, because she won't want them to make Maggie get rid of the animals."

"But won't she call just as soon as the fudge wears off?" asked Tad.

"I'll keep giving her fudge. I know she likes candy."

Nora went up to her room and unlocked her desk drawer. She took one piece of fudge out of the plastic bag and locked the drawer again. Then she put the fudge on a plate and went next door to ring Mrs. Hastings' bell.

Mrs. Hasting was surprised to see her. "I've brought you some fudge," said Nora.

Mrs. Hastings took a good look at the fudge. It had not been improved by its long stay in the desk drawer. It was dry and shriveled and white around the edges.

"It's nice of you, Nora." Mrs. Hastings took another look at the fudge. "But I'm on a very strict diet, and I'm not allowed to eat candy. Thank you anyway." She shut the door.

Nora went home and back to her room. She had to think for a while.

Tad came in to ask her to help him with his homework. Nora showed him where he could find the answers in his book. Then she told him what had happened when she tried to give the fudge to Mrs. Hastings.

"Why don't you mix it with her coffee?" said Tad.

"I'd have to get into her house to do that." Nora heard a scratching in the closet. She opened the closet door just in time to see a little gray mouse squeeze through the crack under the baseboard and disappear.

Of course! Nora thought. There must

be a way to go next door — through the walls. But only a mouse could do that.

Quickly, Nora went to her desk drawer and unlocked it. She took out a piece of fudge. "Can you crush this to a powder, Tad?"

Tad ran out of the room and came back with a hammer. Nora wrapped the fudge in a handkerchief and Tad pounded on it with the hammer.

"What's that banging up there?" Mrs. Cooper was calling up the stairs.

"I'm fixing something," Tad yelled down.

Nora went to the kitchen for a plastic sandwich bag. She put the powdered fudge in it and twisted it into as small a package as she could. Then she tied it with button thread.

Tad watched her. "What are you going to do?"

Nora unlocked the desk drawer again

and took out six pieces of fudge. She gave two pieces to Tad. "Eat them," she said.

Tad started to nibble. He made a face. "It tastes terrible, Nora. Maybe the magic has gone out of it."

"Oh, Tad, we have to *try* it at least. All right then, you don't have to eat the fudge until after I do. Then you'll know if the magic is still working. And you must eat both pieces. Promise!"

"Sure," said Tad. "Now, eat away." He sat down on Nora's bed to watch her.

Nora stood in front of the desk. She shut her eyes tight and thought hard. Then she started to eat the hard old fudge. Nora thought she was going to choke, but she kept right on eating and thinking. First she ate one piece, then two, then three. Nora's nose twitched and suddenly she felt very hungry. It wasn't hard to eat the last piece of fudge.

16

Nora opened her eyes.

What was wrong? Where was she? What were those two strange things? She heard a harsh grating noise. Nora looked up. Now she understood.

The two things in front of her were Tad's feet. The noise was the sound of chewing — a giant chewing. Tad was eating the fudge.

When he finished the second piece, Tad said. "The fudge is still magic all right. You look good as a mouse."

"I'd better not waste time," said Nora. "Tie the bag of powdered fudge around my neck."

Tad tied the little package around Nora's neck with button thread. She ran into the closet and slipped through the crack under the baseboard.

It was dark between the walls, but here and there a crack let in a little daylight. Nora trotted along the mouse trail. It turned and twisted between the rooms, went up and down wooden slats, and traveled into the house next door.

At last Nora saw a hole that would be easy to run through. She came out into the light, blinking her eyes.

Her nose warned her. Something terrible was near!

Nora looked up into two cold blue eyes. Henry! She had gone into Maggie's apartment by mistake!

Without knowing how she did it, Nora turned around and dived back into the mouse hole. Her heart was beating fast. She had to stay very still until it slowed down.

Then Nora went on following the mouse trail. She had to hurry before Mrs. Hastings made that phone call.

Nora poked her head out of a crack and looked all around. She saw the stairs that led down to Mrs. Hastings' part of the house. She slipped out onto the stairs and jumped down, step by step. She wished her feet didn't make such a scratchy sound.

When she reached the hall at the foot of the stairs Nora squeezed under the door into Mrs. Hastings' living room.

Mrs. Hastings was talking on the telephone. "Department of Health? I want to report a dangerous condition. My tenant,

Mrs. Brown, has a great number of animals in her apartment — cats, dogs, birds, snakes, even rats. It smells dreadful. You'll send someone tomorrow? Thank you." Mrs. Hastings gave her address and hung up the telephone.

Nora crouched under the sofa. She was too late! Even if she managed to get the fudge into Mrs. Hastings' coffee, the effect would wear off before tomorrow. Sadly Nora crept out of the room.

She sneaked through Mrs. Hastings' dining room and kitchen and out into the yard. From there it was easy to get into her own yard and creep under the back door into the kitchen.

Tad was sitting at the kitchen table. Nora tugged at his shoelace. Tad looked down. When he saw Nora he picked her up and put her in his shirt pocket. "I don't want Mother to see you," he said. "What happened?"

"Take me to my room," Nora said. "We can talk there."

Tad left the kitchen and went upstairs with Nora in his pocket. "Why didn't you use the fudge?" he asked, untying the packet from Nora's neck.

"Mrs. Hastings was just telephoning the Health Department. I was too late." Nora sat on the pillow and scratched herself. She ran her fingers down her long tail. "Hold me up to the mirror, Tad. I want to see what I look like."

Tad held her in front of the mirror. Nora stroked her whiskers and admired her soft pink ears.

"When are they going to inspect Maggie's apartment?" Tad asked.

"Tomorrow," said Nora.

"That's Saturday. Maggie will be busy feeding people's cats." Tad put Nora back on the pillow. "If we could go over and clean the place, that might help. And maybe we could hide the kittens and the sparrow cage."

"You could turn yourself into a cat and go in the window again. I know a mouse trail to get into Maggie's apartment," Nora said.

"How could we do any cleaning up then?" Tad said. "And if the Health Department people came while we were there, they'd just see two *more* animals. I'm going next door to warn Maggie. She can work some magic herself."

Tad ran out of the room and down the stairs. Nora heard the front door bang as he went out.

17

MRS. COOPER was coming upstairs with an armful of clean laundry. She walked into Nora's room. Nora dived under the pillow, but she wasn't fast enough. Her mother had seen her.

Mrs. Cooper put down the laundry very quietly and lifted the pillow. Nora crouched on the bed, afraid to move. She looked at her mother with frightened eyes. Mrs. Cooper stood quite still, holding the pillow.

Nora looked up at her mother. She knew her mother hated mice. Although she was almost certain her mother would never touch a mouse, Nora decided not to take any chances. She ran to the edge of the bed, shut her eyes, and jumped.

She landed on the hard floor and scuttled under the closet door and through the crack under the baseboard.

"Tad, Tad!" her mother was calling.

"What is it?" yelled Tad from downstairs.

"There's a mouse up here. See if you can catch it."

Tad raced up the stairs. "Where did it go?" he asked Mrs. Cooper.

"Into the closet. I'll get the broom. Maybe we can chase it out." Mrs. Cooper went out.

Tad opened the closet door. "Nora," he whispered.

Nora stuck her head out of the crack. "Yes."

"Maggie's not home. I couldn't warn her. Can you get into her apartment? She keeps an extra door key on the glass tray on her dresser top. If we had her key we could get in and at least clean the apartment."

"Henry's in there," said Nora. "He nearly got me before."

Mrs. Cooper came back into the room with a broom. "Take those shoes out of the closet, Tad," she said. She took a look at a high-heeled shoe with a sparkly buckle. "Where did that come from?"

"It was Maggie's," said Tad.

"Mrs. Brown, Tad." Mrs. Cooper forgot about the mouse and started to examine the contents of the closet. "Are you *sure* Mrs. Brown gave Nora these things? They look too good to give away."

Nora knew that her mother didn't like her to take things from people. She had always told her to say, "No, thank you," when anyone offered her anything.

"Where is Nora, Tad?" Mrs. Cooper was saying.

Nora ran off down the mouse trail away from the closet.

18

NORA wandered along in the half darkness. When she came to a crack or a hole in the wall she put her head to the opening and looked out. One hole gave a fine view of a mousetrap set under the radiator in the bathroom of Nora's house. Another one opened into the hall in Maggie's apartment. Nora could see Lew the lizard sleeping in a doorway. She wondered if mice talked the same language as lizards. She put her mouth to the crack. "Lew," she said as loudly as she could. "Lew, wake up!"

The lizard opened his brown eyes and

stuck out his forked tongue. "Nora," he said, "where are you?"

"Behind the crack in the wall," said Nora. "Lew, I want you to help me."

The big lizard walked over to the crack. "How did you get in there, Nora? It's not big enough for you."

"I turned into a mouse," said Nora. "Lew, can you get the door key off Maggie's dresser?"

"I don't think so," said the lizard. "That's more of a job for Henry."

"See if you can get him to do it, Lew. It's terribly important. Tell him it's to help Maggie."

"All right," said Lew. He went down the hall to the bedroom. In a very short time he came back with the key. "No trouble at all," he said. "That cat is such a showoff."

"Push it through the crack, Lew," said Nora. "And thank you, thank you."

Nora grabbed the door key in her teeth and started back the way she had come. The key was very heavy. Soon she had to put it down and rest.

It was darker now in the space behind the walls, but the cracks glowed brighter. It must be evening, and the lights are turned on, thought Nora.

Once a big mouse bumped against her as he went down the trail. Nora almost dropped the key.

Nora was afraid of getting lost. Then she had an awful thought. What if the magic wore off and she became her old self here between the walls? There wasn't nearly enough room. She'd be squashed.

She tried to hurry, but the key was too heavy. Her teeth were beginning to ache from carrying it.

At last she came to the hole under the bathroom radiator. Nora wiggled through.

She kept as far as she could from the trap. She didn't want to stay under the radiator either. It would be a bad place to suddenly become large.

The bathroom door opened, and Mrs. Cooper came in with some clean towels. Nora moved as quickly as she could. She ran out of the bathroom and down the hall, keeping close to the wall. Her mother came out of the bathroom. "Tad!" she cried. "Here's another mouse. Oh, I wish we could have kept that cat!"

Tad came down the hall. He bent over and took the key. Nora ran to her own room and hid in the closet. She could hear Tad saying, "It got away."

"Did you see which way it went? I'll have to get some more traps." Mrs. Cooper went downstairs.

Tad came into Nora's room. "Nora," he whispered, "where are you?"

"In the closet."

Tad sat on the bed. "Come on out. The coast is clear."

Nora came out. "Put me on the bed. I'm tired."

Tad lifted her onto the bed. Nora burrowed under the covers. "Just don't sit on me," she said.

"Mother's pretty mad at you for taking all that stuff from Maggie. She says some of it's better than what she has herself. And she's looking for you to set the table."

"Couldn't you do it for me? Please, Tad," Nora begged.

"Will you take out the garbage for me?" asked Tad.

"Yes, of course," Nora said.

"O.K. I remember now you said you were going to the library." Tad went out of the room and downstairs.

Nora closed her eyes. It felt so good to be in her own bed. In a minute she was fast asleep.

19

MRS. COOPER was angry. Nora had not come to the supper table at all. After supper her mother found her asleep in her bed. The supper was cold. Mrs. Cooper made Nora eat it anyway.

While she ate, her mother sat at the table across from her and scolded her for taking so many shoes and hats from Maggie Brown.

"But, Mother, she was *glad* to give them to me. They were just cluttering up her closet."

"And now they're cluttering up yours. Tomorrow you are not to go anywhere. I want you to stay home and tidy your room."

"I'll do it in the afternoon, Mother," said Nora. She had to go over to Maggie's apartment and tidy *that* in the morning.

Mrs. Cooper got up from the table. "No, Nora," she said, "I want you to clean your room before you do anything else."

Nora's room was quite small. It was full of all sorts of things. Nora almost never threw anything away. It would take her hours to clean up. She started right after supper, but by bedtime there was still a lot to do.

"Tad," she said, "can you do something about Maggie's place yourself?"

"Of course. What makes you think I need you? I'll spray the rooms with some of that stuff that covers up smells, and I'll hide the animals."

"Sweep the floor, Tad, please," said Nora.

20

NEXT morning after breakfast Tad took Maggie's door key and a spray can and went next door. Nora worked in her room. She kept looking out of her window to see if the man from the Department of Health had come. It would be awful if Tad were still in the apartment when he arrived.

At last Nora finished straightening her room. She shoved a carton of treasures under her bed and jammed her dresser drawers shut. Then she went downstairs and out the front door.

A thin young woman stood on the stoop next door and rang the bell. Mrs. Hastings opened the door.

"I'm Miss Feldman from the Department of Health," said the young woman. "Are you the person who telephoned about animals in an apartment?"

Nora ran over to stand behind Miss Feldman. She had to make some excuse for Tad's being in Maggie's apartment.

Mrs. Hastings was talking. "Yes," she said. "Come in. I'll let you into the apartment upstairs." She turned to Nora. "What is it?"

"I have to tell Tad to come home. He's in Mrs. Brown's apartment," Nora said.

"What's he doing there?" asked Mrs. Hastings.

Nora said the first thing she could think of. "Feeding the cat."

"You see!" said Mrs. Hastings to Miss Feldman. "This woman's business is taking care of people's cats, but she has no time for her own."

Nora felt that she had just made matters worse.

Mrs. Hastings led the way up the stairs. The woman from the Department of Health followed her, and Nora came after.

"Hello," called Mrs. Hastings. "Is anybody home?"

Taffy ran down the hall barking. Miss Feldman took out a notebook and a pen and wrote something down.

Tad came to the top of the stairs and opened the gate. When he saw Nora he grinned and made a funny rumbling noise in his throat. He clenched and un-clenched his hands and scratched them against the bannister.

"Is Mrs. Brown here?" asked Mrs. Hastings. "Miss Feldman would like to see her."

"Maggie's still out cat-sitting," said Tad.

Mrs. Hastings turned to Miss Feldman. "Why don't you take a look around while you're waiting for her?" she said.

"I suppose I might as well," said Miss Feldman. "Where shall I start?"

Nora noticed that the whole apartment smelled of the stuff from the spray can. She thought she liked the zoo smell better.

Mrs. Hastings took Miss Feldman into the living room. Henry the cat met them at the door with a loud meow. Miss Feldman looked at him and made another note in her book.

Suddenly Nora saw Lew. He was standing quite still on one side of a row of books which was propped up on the other side by an iron elephant. The big lizard didn't even blink.

Miss Feldman looked around the room and then went out. She looked into both bedrooms and the bathroom. When she reached the kitchen she said to Mrs. Hastings, "I don't see anything but a cat and a dog. Where are the rats and snakes you called about?"

"They must be hidden somewhere in the apartment," said Mrs. Hastings. She went from room to room, searching in closets, opening drawers, and looking under the furniture.

Nora felt sure Mrs. Hastings would find the other animals, no matter how well Tad had hidden them. Tad was still making that noise in his throat. He stood beside Nora in the kitchen. Now he put his head on one side and rubbed it against Nora's shoulder. Miss Feldman tapped her pen against her notebook. Nora could hear Mrs. Hastings in Maggie's bedroom slamming drawers.

Nora noticed a pan of fudge on the kitchen table. The fudge had been crisscrossed with a knife and cut into pieces. Nora saw that three pieces were missing. So that was what was wrong with Tad!

Nora looked at Miss Feldman. There was no time to lose. Any minute Mrs. Hastings would find the kittens or the sparrow or brush up against Lew. Nora pointed to the pan of fudge. "Mrs. Brown makes the best fudge in the world," she said.

Miss Feldman smiled at Nora. "It looks delicious," she said.

"It sure is delicious," said Tad. Before Nora knew what he was up to, Tad took a piece of fudge and put it in his mouth.

Nora was afraid Tad would bite her if she tried to take the fudge out of his mouth. Before he had time to swallow it, she grabbed him by the shoulders and pushed him out of the kitchen.

"I know Mrs. Brown would want you to have a piece." Nora held up the pan to Miss Feldman.

Suddenly Nora heard a cackle. Miss Feldman jumped.

Maggie was standing in the kitchen doorway. "Please take a piece," she said. "Then you can tell me why you're here."

21

M ISS FELDMAN took a piece of fudge
and ate it.

The next moment Mrs. Hastings rushed
into the room holding a striped yellow
cat by the nape of his neck. At the sight
of Maggie Brown she stopped short and
dropped the cat.

"What a beautiful cat!" said Miss Feldman.

"Do have a piece of fudge, Mrs. Hastings," said the witch.

For a minute Mrs. Hastings couldn't

speak. Then she looked at Nora. "I'm on a diet," she said.

"Just one piece," said Nora. "One piece never hurt anybody."

Maggie smiled. She looked at the yellow cat. "Nora," she said. "You haven't had any of this batch of fudge. Don't you think you should take a couple of pieces?"

Nora took two pieces of fudge and ate them.

Maggie held up the pan to Mrs. Hastings.

Mrs. Hastings looked at the fudge and at Maggie and the yellow cat. She reached for a piece of candy and bit into it. "Delicious!" she said, putting the rest of the fudge in her mouth. She licked her fingers. "That's a handsome cat. Could I have him?"

Nora stooped down and picked up the cat. "I'm sorry, Mrs. Hastings, but he already has a home. I'd better take him back there." She slipped out of the kitchen, ran down the stairs, and out the front door.

Nora sat down on her own front steps with the cat on her lap. Tad wagged his tail. "Why did you have to leave just as things were getting interesting?"

"I wanted to talk to you," said Nora. "What did you do with the rest of the animals?"

"I put the kittens in a shopping bag and hung the bag by a rope out the kitchen window. I was afraid the kittens might jump out. I ate some fudge so I could talk to them. They promised to stay quiet till Maggie could take them back into the house." Tad stretched his neck and looked pleased with himself.

"Well, what made you eat *three* pieces of fudge?" asked Nora.

"I didn't mean to, but you know how it is with that fudge." The cat looked at Nora with wide yellow eyes. "It sure was a mistake. After I'd eaten that third piece, both birds flew out the kitchen window into the tree. They said they wouldn't come back till Maggie came home. They didn't seem to trust *me*." The tip of Tad's yellow tail twitched. "I didn't think that sparrow knew how to fly," he said.

"Where did you get the idea to disguise Lew as a bookend?" Nora wanted to know.

"That was the lizard's own idea," said Tad. "He said he could stand like that for hours. It's just lucky nobody touched him!"

The door of the house next door opened, and Miss Feldman came out on the stoop. She was smiling. "Good-by, Mrs. Brown," she called back over her shoulder. "Remember to save me one of those kittens you told me about."

Tad jumped off Nora's lap and ran up the steps next door and through the open doorway. Nora started to follow him.

Mrs. Hastings was standing inside the door. She was talking to Maggie who leaned over the bannister of the stairs. "Could you give me the recipe for that wonderful fudge?" said Mrs. Hastings.

"I wish I could," said Maggie Brown, "but it's a family secret." The witch rubbed her chin. Then she smiled. "Tell you what I'll do, Mrs. Hastings. I'll give you a piece every day."

Nora stood on the front stoop outside the door. She wondered if Mrs. Hastings would like the animals only part of the day and want to get rid of them the rest of the time. Or maybe she'd get to like them all the time once she started.

Nora heard her mother calling her for lunch. She went back to her own house. "Tad's eating lunch at Mrs. Brown's," she said. "He's been helping her today."

"That's good," said Mrs. Cooper. "I'm glad you children have gotten over that silly notion about Mrs. Brown. You see how right I was when I told you there's no such thing as a witch."